LOOKING AT COUNTRIES

Looking at
POLAND

Kathleen Pohl

Reading consultant: Susan Nations, M.Ed.,
author/literacy coach/consultant in literacy development

Gareth Stevens
Publishing

Please visit our web site at **www.garethstevens.com**.
For a free color catalog describing Gareth Stevens Publishing's list
of high-quality books, call 1-800-542-2595 (USA) or 1-800-387-3178 (Canada).
Gareth Stevens Publishing's fax: 1-877-542-2596

Library of Congress Cataloging-in-Publication Data

Pohl, Kathleen.
 Looking at Poland / Kathleen Pohl ; reading consultant, Susan Nations.
   p. cm. — (Looking at countries)
 Includes bibliographical references and index.
 ISBN-10: 0-8368-9066-3   ISBN-13: 978-0-8368-9066-2 (lib. bdg.)
 ISBN-10: 0-8368-9067-1   ISBN-13: 978-0-8368-9067-9 (softcover)
 1. Poland—Juvenile literature. I. Nations, Susan. II. Title.
DK4040.P56 2008
943.8—dc22   2008005236

This edition first published in 2009 by
Gareth Stevens Publishing
A Weekly Reader® Company
1 Reader's Digest Road
Pleasantville, NY 10570-7000 USA

Copyright © 2009 by Gareth Stevens, Inc.

Senior Managing Editor: Lisa M. Herrington
Senior Editor: Barbara Bakowski
Creative Director: Lisa Donovan
Designer: Tammy West
Photo Researcher: Charlene Pinckney

Photo credits: (t=top, b=bottom, l=left, r=right, c=center)
Cover © Keren Su/Corbis; title page Shutterstock; p. 4 © lookGaleria/Alamy; p. 6 © Momatiuk-Eastcott/Corbis; p. 7t Hellier Robert Harding World Imagery/Getty Images; p. 7b © blickwinkel/Alamy; p. 8t © Paul Springett/Alamy; p. 8b © Caro/Alamy; p. 9 © age fotostock/SuperStock; p. 10 © Jenny Matthews/Alamy; p. 11t © Steve Skjold/Alamy; p. 11b Czarek Sokolowski/AP; p. 12 Piotr Malecki/Getty Images; p. 13t © mediacolor's/Alamy; p. 13b Piotr Malecki/Getty Images; p. 14t © age fotostock/SuperStock; p. 14b © Lech Muszyński/PAP/Corbis; p. 15 © lookGaleria/Alamy; p. 16 © Dallas and John Heaton/Free Agents Limited/Corbis; p. 17t © Atlantide Phototravel/Corbis; p. 17b © Steve Skjold/Alamy; p. 18 © lookGaleria/Alamy; p. 19 Gehman/National Geographic/Getty Images; p. 20t © Ryman Cabannes/photocuisine/Corbis; p. 20b © Barry Lewis/Alamy; p. 21 Krzysztof Dydynski/Lonely Planet Images; p. 22 © JTB Photo Communications, Inc./Alamy; p. 23t © Peter Andrews/Reuters/Corbis; p. 23b © Barbara Ostrowska/PAP/Corbis; p. 24 Kacper Pampel/Reuters/Landov; p. 25t © Grzegorz Momot/PAP/Corbis; p. 25b © Darek Delmanowicz/EPA/Corbis; pp. 26–27 Shutterstock (3)

All rights reserved. No part of this book may be reproduced, stored in a retrieval system, or transmitted in any form or by any means, electronic, mechanical, photocopying, recording, or otherwise, without the prior written permission of the copyright holder.

Printed in the United States of America

1 2 3 4 5 6 7 8 9 11 10 09 08

Contents

Where Is Poland?	4
The Landscape	6
Weather and Seasons	8
Polish People	10
School and Family	12
Country Life	14
City Life	16
Polish Houses	18
Polish Food	20
At Work	22
Having Fun	24
Poland: The Facts	26
Glossary	28
Find Out More	29
My Map of Poland	30
Index	32

Words that appear in the glossary are printed in **boldface** type the first time they occur in the text.

Where Is Poland?

Poland is in central Europe. It shares borders with seven countries. To the west is Germany. To the south are the Czech (chek) Republic and Slovakia. Poland's neighbors to the east are Ukraine, Belarus (beh-luh-ROOS), and Lithuania. In the north, Poland borders Russia. Poland has a **coast** on the Baltic Sea.

Did you know?

Poland is a bit smaller than the state of New Mexico.

Lawmakers meet in the Sejm building in Warsaw, the capital of Poland.

The land boundaries of Poland have changed often over the years. At times, Poland has even disappeared from the map!

Warsaw is the capital. Most of the city was damaged in a war about 60 years ago. Some parts of Warsaw were rebuilt to look as they did in the past. Today, Warsaw is a mix of old castles and modern buildings.

The Landscape

Long stretches of flat land called **plains** make up most of Poland. There are also forests and **bogs**. Bogs are areas of wet, spongy ground. Thousands of small lakes are in the north. Sandy beaches line Poland's coast on the Baltic Sea.

Did you know?

An area of northern Poland is called the "Land of a Thousand Lakes." The lakes formed thousands of years ago, during the Ice Age. Most of northern Europe was covered with ice then.

Rolling farm fields are plowed and planted early in spring.

This peak in the Tatra Mountains is known as the "Sleeping Knight." A tale says the knight will wake up when called to fight for his country.

Bison are the biggest land animals in Europe. At one time, they had almost died out. Now the bison are protected.

Most Polish people, or Poles, live in the central plains. Rolling farmland covers most of that area. Some of the biggest cities are there, too. Warsaw is on the Vistula River. That is the longest river in Poland.

Mountains rise in the southwest. They are the Sudety (soo-DEH-tee) Mountains, the Tatra Mountains, and the Carpathian (kahr-PAY-thee-uhn) Mountains. Many people like to hike in the mountains. Rysy (RIH-see) Peak is the highest point in Poland.

7

Weather and Seasons

Poland has four seasons: winter, spring, summer, and fall. Winters are cloudy and cold, with snow or rain. The coldest months are January and February. Spring is mild—not too hot and not too cold. Summers are warm, and thunderstorms are common. July is usually the warmest and sunniest month. Fall weather is crisp and sunny.

In summer, Poles have fun in the sun! Here, beachgoers relax on the shore of the Vistula River.

Splish splash! Rain is more common in summer than in other seasons.

The snowy mountains of the south are great winter spots for skiing.

The weather is different from region to region. It is mildest on the coast. The coast gets the most sunshine in summer. The weather is cooler and wetter in the mountains. Some peaks are covered with snow most of the year. The lake area in the north is often cloudy.

Did you know?

Zakopane is known as the "winter capital" of Poland. Poles head south to this mountain town to ski.

Polish People

Poland is home to more than 38 million people, called Poles. Almost all of them come from a group of people called **Slavs**. Thousands of years ago, Slavs settled in the area that is now Poland. Today the official language is Polish. It comes from the old language of the Slavs.

Polish people celebrate their past with dance and music. They dance

Did you know?

Wycinanki (vee-chee-NAHN-kee) is the Polish word for "paper cutting." People have decorated their homes with colorful cutouts for more than 200 years.

Girls in folk costumes dance at a festival in Krakow.

People in Poland love fresh flowers. Flowers are sold on every street corner!

Most people in Poland are Roman Catholic. This Catholic church is in the resort town of Zakopane.

the **mazurka** (mah-ZER-kuh) and the polka. At festivals, they dress in colorful folk costumes. In everyday life, most Poles dress as people do in other cities in Europe.

Many Polish people like flowers. They grow flowers, sell them on the streets, and give them as gifts. In spring, some people make paper cutouts in the shapes of flowers.

Religion is very important to the people of Poland. Most of them are Roman Catholics. A few are Protestant, Muslim, or Jewish.

School and Family

Once, only children from rich families in Poland went to school. Today, all children from ages six to 18 must attend. The school year runs from September to June.

Primary school is first. Then children go to a secondary school, called a **gymnasium** (jim-NAY-zee-uhm). They study math, history, and science.

Did you know?

People in Poland celebrate Grandmother's Day and Grandfather's Day in January. Many children make or buy cards and small gifts for their grandparents.

In grades 1 to 3, students usually have one teacher for all their school subjects.

On Sundays, many Polish families enjoy picnics in the park.

This family sits down to talk and share good food at the dinner table.

They learn languages, including English. Some teenagers go to trade schools to learn job skills. Other people go on to college.

Family life is important in Poland. Children, parents, and grandparents might live under one roof. In many families, both parents work outside the home. On Sundays, people go to church and then relax. Families may enjoy a picnic or a walk in a park.

Country Life

More than half of the land in Poland is used for farming. Most farms are small, narrow strips of land. Families live on the farms or in small villages.

Farmers use sharp, curved blades to cut hay. Women and children rake and stack the hay. Horses pull plows in the fields and carts on the roads.

A small village sits among narrow strips of farm fields.

Workers use a tractor and wagon to harvest cabbage.

14

Did you know?

More horses are raised in Poland than in any other country in Europe. People from around the world come to Poland to buy horses.

Poland is known for its fine horses. Arabian horses like these have been bred in Poland for hundreds of years.

Farmers grow grain, sugar beets, potatoes, and cabbages. They raise pigs, beef cattle, and dairy cows, too. Farmers work long hours, and life is hard. Some farmers grow only enough food for their families. Many young people move to cities to find other kinds of jobs.

City Life

Six out of every 10 people in Poland live in big cities. Warsaw is the biggest city. Almost 2 million people live in the capital. It is the center of business and government. Warsaw has new office buildings and tall skyscrapers. It has old town squares and pretty parks. People crowd Warsaw's streets and outdoor markets. They ride buses, **trams**, bikes, or motorbikes to work. Some drive small cars.

People in cities often ride trams, or streetcars, to work. This tram runs along a main street in Warsaw.

Did you know?

Trains connect most of the cities in Poland. It has one of the best train systems in Europe.

People like to feed the pigeons in this square in Krakow. With its many markets and cafés, the main square is a center of activity.

Fresh fruits and vegetables are sold in street markets, such as this one in Krakow.

Krakow, in the south, is another big city. It was once the capital of Poland. Krakow is on the Vistula River. **Tourists** come from all over the world to visit this city.

Gdańsk is a city on the Baltic coast. Ships bring goods in and out of the country at this **seaport**. Factories in Gdańsk make chemicals, machines, food products, and cloth.

Polish Food

Farm families grow most of the food they eat. Many people in Poland eat a lot of meat and vegetables. Cabbage and potatoes are **staples**, or common foods. Beef, sausage, pork, ham, and chicken are popular, too.

Soup is the first course in most main meals. Beet soup is a favorite dish. Bigos (BEE-goss) is a stew made

Did you know?

Ice cream is a favorite dessert in Poland. It is called lody (LUH-dee). Lody shops are common in the cities.

People buy Polish sausages at carts in a Krakow market square.

Beet soup is a favorite dish in Poland. It is served hot or cold.

When the weather is nice, diners crowd outdoor cafés in the cities.

of sausage, cabbage, and mushrooms. Pierogi (puh-ROH-gee), or **dumplings**, are a popular meal, too. They are usually stuffed with meat, cabbage, and mushrooms. Sometimes the filling is cheese, potato, or fruit.

In the cities, people shop at outdoor markets for fresh fruits and vegetables. They eat at cafés and restaurants. Many people enjoy fast foods, such as pizza and hamburgers.

At Work

Many people have service jobs. They may teach school or work in offices and banks. Some workers are doctors or nurses. Others help people at restaurants, hotels, and parks.

Some Poles work in **industry**. They make machinery or build ships. Some people work in factories or steel mills.

Many people in Poland are miners. They work in coal, copper, or salt mines. Coal is Poland's most

Did you know?

People have mined salt near Krakow for 1,000 years. The Wieliczka (veh-LEECH-kah) Mine is like a city deep under the ground. It even has tennis courts and a health clinic!

Each year, more than a million tourists visit this famous salt mine. Its many rooms, including this **chapel**, are carved from salt! A chapel is used for prayer or worship.

Workers build huge ships in Gdańsk, a busy seaport on the northern coast.

Along the Baltic coast, fishing boats set out to catch cod.

important **natural resource**. A natural resource is something supplied by nature and used by people. Coal is burned as fuel. It is also used in making steel.

Most people in the countryside are farmers. Others are loggers, who cut down trees in the forests. Forests cover about one-third of Poland. Many people who live near the coast are fishermen.

Having Fun

People enjoy camping and fishing in Poland. They like to hike and ski in the mountains. They like riding bicycles and horses, too. Sailing on the Baltic Sea is a popular **pastime**. Many people enjoy paddling canoes on the northern lakes, too.

Did you know?

Poland has more than 20 national parks. They are great places for biking and hiking.

Polish people are great sports fans. They crowd the stadiums to watch soccer matches. Kids of all ages enjoy playing soccer. People watch basketball and boxing on television. Polish athletes have competed in the Olympic Games. Many of them have won medals.

Fans crowd a stadium to see a Polish soccer team play a match with Hungary.

Kids everywhere like to play in the snow! Zakopane is a popular place for winter fun.

For hundreds of years, village women have created lacework. They hook thread in fancy patterns to make tablecloths and clothing. They stitch pretty designs on pillows and folk costumes. Men carve wooden boxes and spoons.

In the cities, many Poles go to movies, plays, and festivals. They like all types of music. Classical, jazz, and rock music are popular. Outdoor concerts are common in Warsaw, Krakow, and other cities. People also like to visit museums. They enjoy **operas** and ballets, too.

Dancers perform a ballet at an old castle near Warsaw. Many people in Poland enjoy music and dance.

Poland: The Facts

- Poland became a **republic** in 1918. Its official name is Republic of Poland.

- The president is the **chief of state**. The **prime minister** is the head of the government. Laws are made by the National Assembly. The National Assembly is made up of the Senate and the Sejm.

- Polish citizens who are 18 years of age or older may vote. Presidential elections are held every five years.

- Poland is a very old land that was once ruled by kings.

- Poland joined the European Union in 2004. Member countries of the European Union often work together in areas such as trade and immigration.

The flag of Poland has two bars of red and white. White stands for honesty and kindness. Red stands for bravery.

- Many famous people came from Poland. Marie Curie was born in Warsaw. She made many important discoveries. Frédéric Chopin was a great composer of classical music. Nicolaus Copernicus, a Polish scientist, is known as "the father of astronomy."

Did you know?

The white eagle is the symbol of Poland. When kings ruled Poland long ago, the eagle was shown on the flag.

The unit of money in Poland is the **zloty**. The country is expected to switch to the **euro** within five years.

A flag with a white eagle hangs from a city hall building. The bird is a national symbol of Poland.

Glossary

balcony — an outside porch on an upper floor of a building

bogs — areas of wet land with rotting plants

chapel — a room used for prayer or worship

chief of state — the main representative of a country

coast — an area of land that borders a large body of water, such as an ocean or a sea

concrete — a hard, strong building material

dumplings — dough that is boiled or steamed and sometimes filled with meat, vegetables, or fruit

euro — the unit of money of most countries in the European Union

gymnasium — a secondary school in Poland and some other European countries

industry — a business in which goods or products are made

mazurka — a Polish folk dance

natural resource — something that is supplied by nature and used by people, such as forests and minerals

operas — a play set to music

pastime — a pleasant activity that people do in their spare time

plains — long stretches of flat land

prime minister — the person who handles the day-to-day business of running the government

republic — a kind of government in which decisions are made by the people of the country and their representatives

seaport — a place on the seacoast where ships load and unload goods and passengers

Slavs — group of people who settled in the area of Poland and the Czech Republic thousands of years ago

staples — key foods in a person's diet

tourists — people who visit places for fun

trams — vehicles that transport people on city streets. Trams run on rails or on strong overhead wires.

zloty — the unit of money in Poland

Find Out More

Kids Konnect: Poland
www.kidskonnect.com/content/view/329/27

Encyclopedia FunTrivia: Poland
www.funtrivia.com/en/Geography/Poland-4058.html

Polish-American Heritage: The Art of Polish Paper Cutting
www.info-poland.buffalo.edu/classroom/wycinanki/text.html

Publisher's note to educators and parents: Our editors have carefully reviewed these Web sites to ensure that they are suitable for children. Many Web sites change frequently, however, and we cannot guarantee that a site's future contents will continue to meet our high standards of quality and educational value. Be advised that children should be closely supervised whenever they access the Internet.

My Map of Poland

Photocopy or trace the map on page 31. Then write in the names of the countries, bodies of water, cities, and mountains listed below. (Look at the map on page 5 if you need help.)

After you have written in the names of all the places, find some crayons and color the map!

Countries
Belarus
Czech Republic
Germany
Lithuania
Poland
Russia
Slovakia
Ukraine

Bodies of Water
Baltic Sea
Vistula River

Cities
Gdańsk
Krakow
Warsaw
Zakopane

Mountains
Carpathian Mountains
Rysy Peak
Sudety Mountains
Tatra Mountains

31

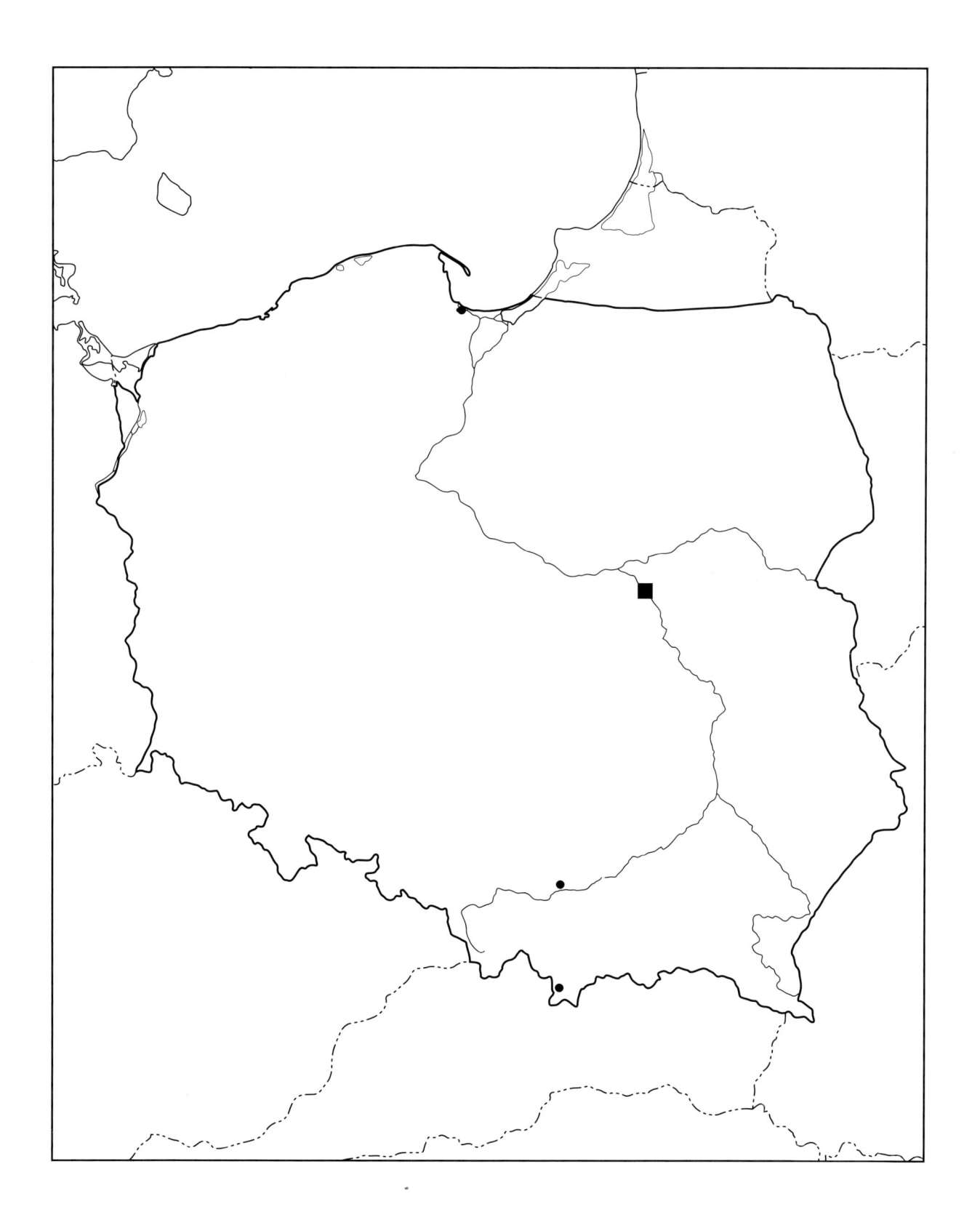

Index

Baltic Sea 4, 17, 23, 24
beaches 6, 8
bison 7
bogs 6

castles 5, 18
cities 7, 15, 16–17, 18, 21
coast 4, 9, 17, 23
countryside 14–15, 19, 23

dance 10, 11, 25

factories 17
families 12–13, 14, 19
farming 6, 7, 14, 15, 23
festivals 10, 11, 25
fishing 23
flag 26
flowers 11
folk dancing 10, 11
foods 13, 14, 15, 17, 20–21
forests 6, 23

Gdańsk 17, 23
government 4, 16, 26
gymnasium 12

horses 14, 15, 24
houses 18–19

industry 22

Krakow 10, 17, 20, 22, 25

lacework 25
lakes 6, 9, 24
landscape 6–7
language 10, 13

mazurka 11
mining 22, 23
money 27
mountains 7, 9, 24
music 10, 25

natural resource 23

operas 25

paper cutting 10
plains 6, 7
polka 11

religion 11, 13, 22

schools 12–13
seaport 17
ships 17, 22, 23
Slavs 10
sports 9, 24

tourists 17, 18, 22
transportation 16, 17

Vistula River 7, 8, 17

Warsaw 4, 5, 7, 16, 18, 25
weather 8–9
white eagle 27
working 13, 22–23

Zakopane 9, 11, 25

32

Looking at Poland